Spooky Texas Tales

Spooky Texas Tales

★

Tim Tingle and Doc Moore

★

Illustrated by Gina Miller

★

Texas Tech University Press

This book is typeset in Sabon. The paper used in this book meets the minimum require-
ments of ANSI/NISO Z39.48-1992 (R1997).

Library of Congress Cataloging-in-Publication Data
Tingle, Tim.
   Spooky Texas tales / Tim Tingle, Doc Moore ; illustrated by Gina Miller.
      p. cm.
   ISBN-10: 0-89672-565-0 (cloth : alk. paper)
   ISBN-10: 0-89672-566-9 (pbk. : alk. paper)
   ISBN-13: 978-0-89672-565-2 (cloth : alk. paper)
   ISBN-13: 978-0-89672-566-9 (pbk. : alk. paper) 1. Ghost stories, American. 2.
Children's stories, American. [1. Ghosts—Fiction. 2. Texas—Fiction. 3. Short stories.] I.
Moore, Doc. II. Miller, Gina, 1981- ill. III. Title.
   PZ7.T489Spo 2005
   [Fic]—dc22   2005009474

Printed in the United States of America

05 06 07 08 09 10 11 12 13 / 9 8 7 6 5 4 3 2 1
SB

Texas Tech University Press
Box 41037
Lubbock, Texas 79409-1037 USA
800.832.4042
ttup@ttu.edu
www.ttup.ttu.edu

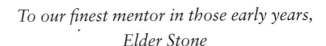

To our finest mentor in those early years,
Elder Stone

Contents

Acknowledgments

For inspiring and even overwhelming us with us with their unique renderings of their favorite ghost stories, we would like to extend our immense gratitude to Elizabeth Ellis, Len Cabral, David Holt, Tom McDermott, Finley Stewart, Jackie Torrence, Connie Regan-Blake, Harriet Lewis, J. J. Reneaux, Dennis Frederick, Jeannine Pasini Beekman, and Richard and Judy Dockery Young.

Folkorists and story collectors Dr. John Davis, Rosemary Davis, Dr. John O. West, Dr. Juan Sauvageau, and writers Zinita Fowler, Docia Williams, and Ed Syers have made important contributions to the spiritual well-being of ghosts throughout Texas, and on their behalf we thank you.

The above-mentioned list of writers and performers is, of course, incomplete, for the river of ghosts and those who speak of them is deep and wide. Thanks to you all. And lest we forget the day-to-day workers in the fight for literacy, we thank the teachers and librarians who strive to promote better storytelling and writing.

We are forever indebted to the administrative and editorial staff at Texas Tech University Press, who continue to be patient, learned, and a joy to work with, especially Judith Keeling.

Tailybone

A long time ago in the Big Thicket of East Texas there lived an old man in a log cabin all by himself. He had built that cabin with a fireplace across one wall. He'd collected and laid every stone, all by himself. He'd cut and fit every log, all by himself. And when he was hungry, he'd go out and hunt all day long, all by himself.

If he caught anything, he'd bring it home and cook it right there in the fireplace. If he didn't catch anything, he would cook himself up a big ol' pot of beans.

One evening, the old man was sitting in his rocking chair by the fireplace cooking those beans. He was rocking back and forth, coasting in and out, not paying any attention to what was going on. Every half hour, he would reach over and stir those beans.

After a while, he saw something move back in the corner of the cabin, back where there was a hole in the floor. He should have fixed the hole months ago, but he just hadn't gotten around to it.

Something was sticking its head up through that hole. It was the ugliest looking thing he'd ever seen! It had little ol' beady red eyes, sharp-pointed ears, and teeth that looked like they had never seen a Colgate toothbrush. It scared that old man something awful.

"If that thing comes in here, I'm gonna cut it," he said to himself.

And it did. It came right up out of the hole and circled the room once, then twice. The third time around the old man drew back his hatchet and threw it. It chopped that thing's tail right off.

The critter went on back through the hole and ran across the yard and into the pasture, across the pasture and into the woods, making the most awful sound you ever heard.

Yeeeek! Gummy! Yeeeek! Gummy! Yeeeek!!

The old man spit on his dirty windowpane and rubbed a clean hole big enough to see through. When the thing had finally disappeared into the woods, he turned back to the room. And there he saw it—that old tail just wiggling back and forth, back and forth, on the cabin floor. He picked it up and took a look.

"Not enough meat to eat. Fur's too scraggly for a coat collar," he said.

Then he had an idea. He took the tail over to the fireplace and nailed it up on the wall for decoration. You know how some men are about their hunting decorations. Then he went back to the fireplace and cooked those beans right on down.

When they were ready, he got himself a big bowl and spooned it up full. And he ate every bite! Then he spooned himself another bowl full and ate that too. The old man didn't stop till there wasn't a bean left in that pot. Then he got himself some of yesterday's cornbread and sopped up the juice.

The old man looked at that cooking pot. "Cleaner than it was when I started," he said. So he put it up in the pantry just like it was.

The old man had worked around the cabin for about an hour when he started to get a tummy ache. He decided to go to bed early. Now, he had a big feather bed in one corner of the cabin. He fell back in it, pulled a quilt up around his neck, a quilt his momma had made for him a long time ago, and went off sound asleep.

After a few hours he heard a noise on the wall outside the cabin. *Screeech!* Then he heard a voice.

"Tailybone, tailybone. I want my tailybone."

It scared that old man. He kept some dogs under the porch and he called those old dogs out.

"Ino, Uno, Comptico Calico!" He called them that

'cause that's what their names were. "Get after that thing!"

And they did.

They chased that old thing across the yard and into the pasture, across the pasture and into the woods. Those dogs were howling something terrible.

Ow, ow, ow, ow, ooow!

That thing was making the most awful sound you ever heard.

Yeeeek! Gummy! Yeeeek! Gummy! Yeeeek! Yeeeek! Yeeeek!

When the old man couldn't hear those dogs or that thing anymore, he went back into the cabin. He put an extra bar across the door and fell back into that feather bed. He pulled that quilt up around his neck, that quilt his momma had made for him a long time ago.

The old man went off sound asleep, but it wasn't long before he heard it again, a noise up over the door.

Screeech!

That thing was back! This time it was trying to get in through the door. It scared that old man. He listened real close, and he heard it again.

"Tailybone, tailybone. I want my tailybone."

The old man called his dogs out again. "Ino, Uno, Comptico Calico! Get after that thing!"

And they did. They chased that thing across the yard and into the pasture, across the pasture and into the woods, howling all the way.

Ow, ow, ow, ow, ooow!

That thing was making the most awful sound you ever heard.

Yeeeek! Gummy! Yeeeek! Gummy! Yeeeek! Yeeeek! Yeeeek!

When he couldn't hear his dogs or that thing anymore, he went back into the cabin and put another bar on the door just for safety. He went over and fell back in that feather bed and pulled that quilt up around his neck, that quilt his momma had made for him a long time ago. But this time he couldn't get to sleep. He tossed and he turned; he turned and he tossed.

Before he could even get one eye closed, he heard it, way off in the distance. He didn't know if it was the wind blowing through those East Texas pine trees or maybe just the wind blowing around the outside of that log cabin. He listened real close and thought he heard somebody calling off in the distance.

"Tailybone, tailybone! I'll GET my tailybone!"

This time that old man was really frightened. He didn't know what to do first. He built up a big old fire in the fireplace so nothing could come down the chimney. He put another bar on the door. He closed the window shutters tight. He rolled that quilt up, that quilt his momma had made for him a long time ago, rolled it into a ball and forced it down the hole in the floor. He got a big old rock he kept there in the cabin. You never know when you might need a rock. He put that rock on top of the quilt.

The old man should have felt safe and secure, but he didn't.

He picked up his hatchet and spent the rest of the night just walking, swinging, and thinking; thinking, walking, and swinging. He knew if he could stay up till daylight, he could deal with that thing.

When he thought he had been up long enough, he went over and peeked though a crack in the wall. He saw some sunlight out there, so he opened the shutters. That sun came in and felt so good. He was so relaxed and comfortable, he threw open the window and let the breeze come in.

Then he headed straight for that feather bed. He fell back in it and said to himself, "I'm gonna get me a good night's sleep if I have to take it in the daytime!"

But you know what happened? Right there on the foot of the bed, that thing showed up again. It had come in through the open window. And you know what it said?

"Tailybone, tailybone! I want my tailybone."

"Your old tailybone's a-hanging over there on the wall by the fireplace," the old man said. "If you want it, go get it!"

And you know, that thing did.

When it did, the old man jumped out of the window. He ran across the yard and into the pasture, across the pasture and into the woods. Ain't nobody seen or heard tell of him since.

Now, folks, if you went into the Big Thicket of East Texas tonight and started looking for that log cabin, you wouldn't find it. It's long gone. But if the moon was shining and the breeze blowing, you could find that fireplace.

And if you go out there and stand by that fireplace, long about ten o'clock tonight, stand there in the moonlight and listen—way off in the distance you'll hear it. In a while you can make out the words.

"Tailybone, tailybone! I GOT my tailybone!"

And that's the story of the East Texas Tailybone.

The Golden Arm

Aaron Dalhart loved his two-thousand-acre family farm and the white frame house that went with it. It was, after all, the house he was raised in, he and his two brothers and four sisters. Everybody who knew Aaron knew of his obsession with his house and river-bottom acreage.

On the day she met Aaron, Estelle Bonnet told him she would take her final ride in a hearse before she would visit him in his little white house.

"I just don't like white all that much," she said. "It seems too awful ordinary."

So nobody expected the two would even be friends, much less be married a month after they met. But then, nobody understood the power of Estelle's arm—the Golden Arm.

Aaron took the next week off for the sole purpose of painting his house blue. He cleaned the cobwebs and dirt-dauber nests from under the eaves. He scraped the loose paint and washed the house clean. His friends and neighbors made excuses to drive by Aaron's house, just to watch him stand on his stepladder and paint.

Aaron was readying his house to receive his first lady guest in twenty years. As the men who gathered on the courthouse square used to say, "Estelle didn't come from around here." While her uncle, Bob Watson, came from a long line of hard-working local residents, Estelle was new to town. Though Bob never spoke of it, the downtown gossip was that Estelle had appeared unexpectedly on the ten o'clock bus from Abilene.

"She come all the way from Callie-for-nigh-yea," Old Man Jackson said. "Purty as a pup with them blue eyes and her blond hair. Not like no Watson I ever seed."

According to the story, after the bus unloaded she stood in a long line waiting to use the telephone to call her uncle Bob. "After maybe a half hour," said Old Man Jackson, "she pulled the sleeve of her blouse up so's everybody in line could get a look at her arm—the Golden Arm. Well, that's all it took. The fellar using the phone just hung up right in the middle of a sentence. Everybody else backed off, way off, and let her use the phone."

"You see," he continued, "nobody in town had never seen no golden arm before. From somewhere above her elbow all the way down to the fingers of her right hand, her arm was solid gold."

The first time Aaron saw Estelle, she was standing at the mailbox in front of the Watson place. Aaron was driving his pickup truck, on his way to town to buy seed and fertilizer. Out of the corner of his eye, he saw her. He was absent-mindedly guiding the steering wheel with one hand and fumbling with the radio knob with the other.

When Aaron saw Estelle lift her right arm, the Golden Arm, to open the mailbox, he drove his truck into the ditch on the opposite side of the road. His front fender smacked up against a cottonwood tree.

"You alright?" Estelle hollered.

Aaron climbed out of his truck and surveyed the damage before replying.

"Yeah. My truck's bent up a little. But I'm alright."

"Come on over and call a wrecker from the house," she said. "I'll make you some iced tea while you wait."

Ten minutes later Aaron sat on the front steps, and Estelle occupied the porch swing behind him. That's when the famous conversation took place, the conversation resulting in Aaron painting his house blue. It went more or less like this:

Aaron gulped down his glass of tea without saying a word.

"Can I get you some more tea?" asked Estelle.

"That'd be nice of you," said Aaron.

When she returned from the kitchen with the full glass, Aaron said, "Why don't you come over to my place for supper? You and your uncle can both come. I'll kill a couple of fryers and we can have fried chicken. I cook good fried chicken and potato salad, too. I don't do desserts."

"Aaron, we just met."

"I said bring your uncle."

"Why, Aaron Dalhart, I would take my final ride in a hearse before I'd be caught dead in your little white house. That is, of course, unless you painted it, prettied it up some."

"What color?" asked Aaron.

"The color of my eyes," Estelle said, lifting her golden right arm and brushing the hair from her face. "Come get a good look."

That's all it took.

Two weeks later, Aaron and Estelle were married. Everybody in town showed up for the wedding. Some came to get a look at the woman who finally lassoed Aaron after sixty years of bachelorhood. Most came to get a look at the Golden Arm.

Following the wedding, folks noticed many changes around the Dalhart place. Flowers appeared on the front porch. Flowerbeds and flowering bushes soon surrounded the house. When Johnny Mayhan, a schoolmate of Aaron's, saw Aaron painting his barn blue, he pulled his truck to the roadside and watched for twenty minutes. When Aaron waved to him, he just shook his head in wonder and drove away.

While it's true that Aaron had, in the ten years previous to their marriage, fewer visitors than a recent widow has fits of laughter, nobody came to see Aaron and Estelle. Nobody was invited, and nobody came. And that was fine with Aaron. He knew his old friends would make fun of the way he waited on Estelle hand and foot. But it wasn't her hands or her feet Aaron was interested in. It was her arm—the Golden Arm. Aaron couldn't take his eyes off it.

One night Estelle fell asleep in front of the fireplace. Aaron tiptoed behind her and stood for the longest time, staring at the arm. After almost half an hour, Aaron stoked up the courage to touch the arm, lightly, just at the wrist.

Estelle jumped, and Aaron was so startled he fell over backward.

When Estelle first took sick, the folks in town assumed it had something to do with her arm. They were correct. Her left arm, the flesh and blood one, had been bitten by a brown recluse spider. Descended from a long line of brown recluse spiders living under the roof overhang of Aaron's front porch, the spider that bit Estelle had no choice but to move into the attic when Aaron painted the house. No one could really blame the spider. She had her own family to think of.

Doctor Moore, the town physician, was less than hopeful about Estelle's chances of surviving the spider bite. For years, Doctor Moore had joked, "I'm not the kind of doctor that can do you any good."

In this case he was right. Estelle died a week after the spider danced down her web from the attic in search of something to feed all those kids.

On the evening of her death, Estelle said to Aaron, "Please bury my arm with me. Promise me you'll bury my Golden Arm. I want it in the coffin with me."

"Don't talk like that," he said. "You are going to be fine."

"I am dying, Aaron. Just make me this one promise."

"Alright. I promise to bury your Golden Arm with you." Aaron then buried his face in his hands and wept for an hour. When he looked up from his crying, Estelle was dead.

Everybody in town showed up for the funeral. Some came for a final look at the woman who'd died after rescuing Aaron from sixty years of bachelorhood. Most came to get a final look at the Golden Arm.

Hundreds of curious onlookers paraded by the coffin.

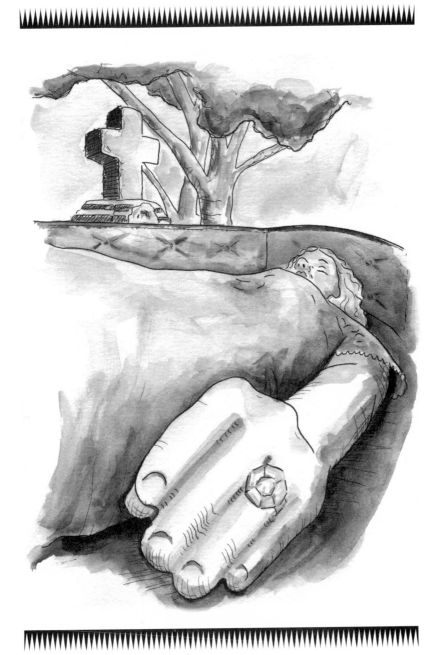

Estelle looked sweet as a slumbering child. Her left arm was bent at the elbow, and across the waist of her baby blue dress lay the Golden Arm. For the entire service Aaron stood at the head of the coffin. His eyes moved up and down the arm, following the tapering of the wrist, studying every curve of the golden fingers.

Aaron rode with the coffin to the cemetery, insisting that it remain open till the very moment of the burial. Townspeople turned away in embarrassment to see his covetous eyes wrap themselves around the Golden Arm.

"Looks to me like he grieves for that arm more than he does his bride," Old Man Jackson was heard to say. "Not that it's any of my business." Privately, of course, he considered everything that happened in town to be his business.

On his first night alone after the funeral, Aaron paced the floor for hours. Finally, unable to spend a single evening without the precious arm, he threw a shovel in the back of his truck and drove to the cemetery.

The ground above Estelle was soft and unsettled. In less than an hour Aaron had completely uncovered the wooden box. He leaned over the edge of the grave and pried open the lid of the coffin with the blade of his shovel. Carefully lowering himself into the hole, Aaron gripped the Golden Arm just below the elbow.

He was surprised at how easily it pulled away. He held

the arm high, lifting it above the ground. A dazzling sight appeared before him. The round yellow moon and silver stars were reflected in the Golden Arm. Aaron shivered with delight.

"Now, at last, you are mine," he said.

Once again home, Aaron laid the arm in Estelle's favorite chair. He built a small fire in the fireplace. He moved his own chair close enough so he could watch the firelight flicker on the Golden Arm.

Suddenly, in the flames reflected on the arm, he saw Estelle. She smiled at first but then cast her gaze to the stub of her right arm. Her smile slowly turned to a scowl, and she said, "Who's got my Golden Arm?"

Aaron leapt to his feet and whirled about the cabin. Seeing nothing, he grabbed the arm and retreated to his bedroom. Clutching the arm to his chest, he climbed into bed. Exhaustion and the stress of the day finally caught up with Aaron, and he was soon snoring loudly.

Aaron didn't know how long he slept, but he knew it wasn't more than an hour. He was awakened by a tapping sound on his windowpane, followed by Estelle's voice.

"Who's got my Golden Arm?"

He jumped to his feet and ran to the window. No one was there. He saw only the full moon in a clear sky and acres of cotton fields. Over his shoulder Aaron thought he heard the front door opening. Estelle's voice now came from the living room.

"Who's got my Golden Arm?"

Footsteps crossed the floor. Aaron froze. His eyes moved to the doorknob. The knob was slowly turning.

He gripped the arm by the wrist and fled to the closet, easing the door shut. He backed against the hanging pants and shirts, clinging to the arm. Over his shoulder he heard the voice, as if it came from the wall behind him.

"Who's got my Golden Arm?"

Aaron flung open the closet door, and there stood Estelle, pointing at him with the stump of her right arm.

"YOU'VE GOT IT!"

Aaron Dalhart was discovered the next morning by the groundskeeper of the cemetery. "The poor man went plumb mad," Old Man Jackson later recalled. "It looked like he musta dug her up the night before. At least that's what the sheriff said, the way the dirt was covered with dew moisture. Cain't nobody really tell, I don't think."

"By the time Billy Vickers found him, he was trying to cover her up again. Shoveling dirt right down on her open coffin. And she looking so purty otherwise, with that blond hair, that baby blue dress, and that Golden Arm."

The Hairy Man

Wiley and his mama and daddy lived in a small cabin on the Brazos River. Wiley's daddy, some say, was a bad man. They say he could steal, lie, and cheat along with the best of 'em. They say he would gamble all night long if he got a chance.

One morning Wiley's daddy left. He said he was going fishing, but he did not return that evening. This was not unusual. Often Wiley's daddy did not return in the evenings.

The next day, Wiley's daddy's boat washed up on the shore. A neighbor found it and put out the word for everyone to come to Wiley's house. That afternoon, some fifteen men set out in their boats, looking up and down the Brazos, trying to locate Wiley's daddy.

On the third evening they heard a laughing sound back in the cedar brakes.

"Ha, haaa, haaaa, haaaaa!"

They knew that sound. It was the Hairy Man. Quick as they could, they turned their boats around and headed home. They wanted nothing to do with the Hairy Man.

From that day on, Wiley's mama would say, "Wiley, the Hairy Man's done got your daddy. He's gonna get you if you don't watch out."

"Oh, I'll watch out," said Wiley. Wiley always minded his mama. "I'll have my dogs with me. You know the Hairy Man can't stand them dogs."

Now Wiley's mama had lived on the Brazos for many years, she and her family before her. She was a conjuring woman. She could witch for water, run rattlesnakes off—do all the conjuring she thought needed to be done. She'd taught Wiley some of it too.

One day Wiley's mama told him to go into the cedar brakes and cut some poles for the new chicken roost.

"You take your hound dogs, Wiley. And look out for the Hairy Man." And Wiley did, 'cause Wiley always minded his mama.

Wiley was walking through the cedars when a small pig ran between his legs. The dogs took off, chasing after it. That scared Wiley. He kept an eye to his front, an eye to his back, an eye to his right, and an eye to his left.

"I don't want that Hairy Man slipping up on me, me being without my dogs and all," said Wiley, chopping poles like his mama told him to.

Then Wiley saw him, off in a clump of trees—the Hairy Man.

The Hairy Man grinned a terrible grin at Wiley. Wiley saw his big, red eyes, his hairy body, and his dirty teeth. Wiley was scared. You would be, too. But he didn't let on. Uh-uh.

"You quit grinnin' at me! And stay just where you are," Wiley said to the Hairy Man.

But the Hairy Man kept grinnin' and started coming toward Wiley. Wiley saw the Hairy Man's feet were like cow's feet, and he was dragging a gunnysack.

"Ain't never seen a cow climb a tree," thought Wiley. And up a little scrub oak Wiley went.

"Why you run from me?" asked the Hairy Man.

"My mama told me to stay away from you," said Wiley. And you know Wiley always minded his mama.

"Whatcha got in that old gunnysack?" asked Wiley.

"Nothing yet," said the Hairy Man.

"Get on out of here," cried Wiley.

"Believe I'll stay!" said the Hairy Man, grabbing his ax and going to work chopping that little scrub oak. The Hairy Man sang,

*"Chop, chop. Down come a tree.
Chop, chop. Down come a tree."*

But Wiley thought up his own song, and he sang it out loud.

*"Back to the tree, big old chips.
Back to the tree, big old chips."*

The chips jumped right back where they came from.

Still, the Hairy Man was gaining on Wiley. Then, off in the distance, Wiley heard his dogs.

"Those are my dogs!" said Wiley.

"Nope," said the Hairy Man, grinnin' his terrible grin. "I sent a wild pig through here a while back. Your dogs took off after him."

"I know my dogs," said Wiley. "They're coming back. Here, doggies!"

The noise got closer.

"You know I can't stand them dogs," said the Hairy Man, and off he ran into the cedar brakes.

Wiley climbed on down and set out for home, carrying the poles his mama needed, with his dogs following along behind. He told his mama everything that had happened to him.

"Wiley, that's just the first time. You gotta fool the Hairy Man three times before you're safe. Next time, here's

what you do," and she leaned over and whispered something in his ear.

"Don't make much sense," thought Wiley. But he didn't say it out loud. He just told his mama he would do exactly what she said. After all, Wiley always minded his mama.

The next morning, after tying his dogs up with a good stout rope, Wiley went back to the cedar brakes. He hadn't walked long before, right around the bend in the road, he saw the Hairy Man. He was grinning that terrible grin and holding a gunnysack.

"Hello, Hairy Man," said Wiley.

"Hello, Wiley," said the Hairy Man, opening his gunnysack.

"Hairy Man," said Wiley, "my mama said you are one of the best conjurers on the river. Is that true?"

"Not one of the best, Wiley. I am the best!"

"I'll bet you can't turn yourself into a skunk."

"Watch this," said the Hairy Man. He jumped up and turned himself around once in the air. And when he landed, there stood a skunk. Wiley's eyes grew big, but he knew what to do.

"That was too easy," said Wiley. "Bet you can't turn yourself into a raccoon."

The skunk looked at Wiley, then jumped up and turned himself around once in the air. And when he landed, there stood a raccoon.

"You're pretty good," said Wiley. "But I heard about a

man that could turn himself into a baby possum. You better not try that. You're too big for that one."

The raccoon just laughed a Hairy Man laugh and jumped up and turned himself around once in the air. And when he landed, there stood a baby possum.

Wiley grabbed the baby possum and stuffed it into the gunnysack. Then he took off one of his shoestrings, tied the sack real tight, and threw it in the deepest part of the river, and off he ran toward home.

Before he'd run half a mile, there in the middle of the path stood the Hairy Man, grinning his terrible grin.

"How'd you do that?" said Wiley.

"Easy," said the Hairy Man. "I just turned myself into the North Wind and blew myself right out of that sack."

"You're good," said Wiley. "Real good." But Wiley was stalling for time. His mama's help had run out, and Wiley was on his own.

"If you're such a good conjuring man," said Wiley, "can you make things disappear?"

"That's my special skill," said the Hairy Man.

"Show me something," said Wiley.

"Zipppp!" said the Hairy Man, and Wiley's shirt flew off his back and wrapped around a tree. The long sleeves even tied themselves neatly around the trunk.

"Not bad," said Wiley. "But that was just a regular old shirt. My mama said some conjuring over this rope I got for a belt. See if you can make it disappear."

"I'll do better than that," said the Hairy Man. "All the rope in the county, disappear!"

Wiley's rope belt disappeared, and his pants fell down to his ankles. He pulled 'em up, all the while shouting, "Here, doggies. Come get yourself the Hairy Man! Here, doggies!"

With the ropes that Wiley had tied them with gone, the dogs came running.

"You know I can't stand those dogs," cried the Hairy Man, and off he ran.

When Wiley got home he told his mama everything he had seen.

"That's twice you have fooled the Hairy Man, Wiley. But you gotta fool him three times." His mama made a big pot of coffee and sat down to think how they would fool him again. She slow-sipped her coffee and thought.

"Wiley, go get that baby pig from the sow. Clean him up and bring him to me." Wiley, of course, did as he was told. Wiley always minded his mama.

"Now, Wiley. Go hide in the attic and be very quiet."

And Wiley did.

And Wiley was.

In a few minutes, the Hairy Man came clomping down the road and stomping on their porch.

"I've come for your baby, ma'am," the Hairy Man said.

"You won't get my baby," Wiley's mama said, sipping her coffee like nothing was happening.

"Better give him to me, or I'll dry up your well," said the Hairy Man.

"I'll make it rain and fill again this very night," said Wiley's mama.

"Then I'll make the boll weevils attack your cotton."

"Hairy Man, you wouldn't do that. That would be too mean, even for you," said Wiley's mama.

"Oh, I guess I am about the meanest man you've ever seen," said the Hairy Man.

"I don't know about that," thought Wiley's mama, just to herself. Then she said, "If I give you my baby, will you leave everyone else here alone forever and a day?"

"I can do that."

"Then come on in," said Wiley's mama. "My baby is under the bed covers."

The Hairy Man pulled back the covers.

"There's nothing here but a pig!"

"That's right," said Wiley's mama. "But it's a baby pig, and it belongs to me, so it's my baby. Now take it and go, like you promised."

The Hairy Man frowned, and Wiley's mama located both double-up fists on her hips and reminded him, "Remember, if you don't keep your word, you will lose all your conjuring power."

The Hairy Man hollered.

The Hairy Man stomped.

The Hairy Man said bad words.

Then he ran out the door, breaking everything in sight.

"Is the Hairy Man gone, Mama?" asked Wiley.

"Yes, Wiley, he's gone from here. And he will never return. We have fooled the Hairy Man three times."

Neither Wiley nor his mama ever saw the Hairy Man ever again, but here lately some of the cedar choppers say they've seen the Hairy Man. They say he still hangs out in those cedar brakes, still doing his meanness.

But the smart ones say that if you do like Wiley, if you always mind your mama, you have nothing to worry about. That's what the smart ones say.

Prom Queen

Tommy was an all-state quarterback for Alice High School's football team. Sherry, his steady girlfriend, was the head cheerleader. They'd been going together for four years and already had their lives planned. They would attend a small college, Texas A&I in Kingsville. After graduation, they would return home to Alice, where Tommy would coach football and Sherry would teach English.

But those plans never came to be.

The trouble first started two weeks before the senior prom. Sherry told Tommy she really didn't want to go to the prom in his pickup truck because she might get her new prom dress dirty. Tommy was more hurt than mad. He'd rebuilt that truck and was proud of it.

"I talked my father into letting us take his new car to the prom," Sherry said.

"I'm not about to drive your father's car," said Tommy. "What if someone parks too close and scratches it? No way! We'll ride in my truck."

Well, both Tommy and Sherry assumed the other would finally give in. But they didn't. In fact, they dug their heels in, stubborn as the dirt they lived on.

A week before the prom, Sherry told Tommy she wanted the largest corsage of anybody in school, a dozen flowers. Tommy had planned on a more modest corsage, leaving enough money to eat out after the dance.

"We can drive to San Antonio, go someplace nice," he said. Sherry turned away, silent and mad.

Friday morning before the prom, Sherry met Tommy at his locker. She held his football jacket in front of her, neatly folded. Sitting on top of it was his senior ring. "I've already found another date to the prom," Sherry said, handing him his jacket and his ring.

At that moment Tommy's whole world came crashing down around him. By lunchtime, the whole school knew about it. His football friends made him promise to come to the dance anyway. "It might be the last time we're together as a football team," someone said.

Saturday evening Tommy found himself driving his truck

to the prom. He was wearing a rented tuxedo, with a small corsage on the seat next to him. As he approached the entrance to the gym, he saw couples lining up to have their photos taken in front of a tropical backdrop.

Rather than stand in the line alone, he decided to take a country drive and return to the dance later. He drove fifteen miles down dusty roads lined with mesquite trees. He then parked his truck and watched the evening stars pop out. As he leaned against a front fender, the metal still warm from the hot Texas sun, Tommy thought about his future without Sherry.

When he glanced at his watch, he realized it was getting late. He thought he should return to the dance. As he backed his truck to turn around, his headlights caught something standing in the shadows. He parked and stepped over the shallow ditch at the road's edge.

In lacy shadows cast by the moon on the mesquite trees, he saw a beautiful girl in a white prom dress.

"What are you doing here?" Tommy asked. "What are you doing out here in the brush so dressed up?"

She looked up and shyly replied, "Well, you might not believe it, but I was hoping to get a date to the prom."

Tommy laughed. "That's the most ridiculous thing I've ever heard. Standing out in the middle of nowhere, dressed to go to the prom!" Then he remembered his own situation. "Well, I've got a corsage. Would you like to be my date?"

"Why, yes," she said. "My name is Julie. I would be honored to accompany you to the prom."

Tommy offered her his arm and helped her into his truck. "Would you like this corsage?"

"How nice of you," she said.

He tried to fasten the flowers to her dress but jabbed the pin into his thumb instead. He expected her to tease him like Sherry would have done. She only smiled and said, "Here, let me help you."

As they drove slowly into town, he kept glancing at her, trying to think of something to say. He found himself blushing like a seventh grader on his first date. She finally broke the silence, saying, "You have a beautiful truck."

When they arrived at the gym, the parking lot was packed, and they had to park a half-mile away. Arm in arm, they walked in silence, in hushed anticipation of the evening. They entered the dance just as the fast music was over and the slow dance music was starting up.

"Would you like to dance?" he said.

"Yes."

As they stepped onto the dance floor, Julie did something Tommy would never forget. She held his hand over her head and did a beautiful little turn as she came into his arms. It was so old-fashioned and sweet.

They danced slowly, even holding each other close as one song ended and they waited for another to begin. Soon

the dance was over, and the lights came up. Tommy's football friends were curious about his new date, but when they saw that special smile on Tommy's face, they decided to leave the two of them alone.

On the drive home, Tommy began to make new plans for his life, irrational plans. He barely knew who Julie was. When they reached the driveway leading to her home and he turned into the drive, Julie grabbed the steering wheel. It was the first and only abrupt thing he ever saw her do.

"No! No!" she shouted.

"What is it?" he asked.

"Oh, I'm sorry. But my parents are still up. They'll invite you in and make a pot of coffee. It'll spoil the mood. I want it to be just like this. Please, let me walk the rest of the way."

"Fine," he said, draping his football jacket over her shoulders to keep the chill off. He watched as she walked down the long driveway. The porch light came on, and she disappeared inside.

Tommy's heart pounded with a thrill he hadn't felt since his last touchdown of the season. He hopped back into his truck and sped to town. He could barely sleep that night.

At five thirty the next morning, he drove to the truck stop and tossed down a quick cup of coffee. By six fifteen he was parked on the road in front of Julie's house.

Then he came to his senses. "I can't show up knocking

on her door at this hour in the morning. I don't even know her parents." So he drove back to the truck stop and ordered a big platter of scrambled eggs and bacon.

At eight o'clock, a more decent hour, he turned down the driveway to Julie's house. The closer he came, the older and more run-down the house seemed to be. When he knocked on the screen door, one of the hinges popped off. He paused, then knocked again for several minutes. The door slowly creaked open. The wrinkled face of an old woman appeared.

"Go away," the woman said. "You cruel boy. Go away! Leave me alone!"

She slammed the door. Tommy, wondering who she thought he was, started banging on the window. Ten minutes later, when the old woman opened the door again, he stuck his boot inside so she couldn't close it.

"What do you want?" she asked.

"I want to see Julie."

"Oh, you've come here to see Julie. All right, I'll show you Julie." She ushered him into a dark living room and gestured to the fireplace.

"There's Julie! Now, you can leave."

"What do you mean? I want to see her," he said.

The old woman shuffle-stepped to the fireplace. She reached for a picture above the mantel and handed it to him. It was a yellow photograph in a faded wooden frame.

The smiling girl in the picture looked very much like Julie.

"This must be you as a young girl," he said. "Where's Julie? I'm not leaving till I see her."

"Well, I guess I've got to show you Julie." She led him out the back door and into a small garden. In the rear of the garden, she stepped aside, allowing Tommy to open a rusty wrought-iron gate. They marched through a clump of catclaw bushes and finally stood in an old cemetery. The woman knelt down.

"Here's Julie."

On the gravestone Tommy saw her full name, Julie Elizabeth Forestner. He saw first the date of her birth and then noted the date of her death at the age of sixteen years. But the date of her death was fifty years ago. Tommy stood up in disbelief.

"This can't be true. I took her to the prom last night. This can't be happening."

"Julie was my daughter," the old woman said. "She was struck by a car in front of the house. She was waiting for her prom date. That was fifty years ago this weekend."

As Tommy backed away, he saw something colorful at the base of the gravestone. Kneeling down, he spread the weeds apart. There, neatly folded, was his football jacket. He slung the jacket over his shoulder.

"I won't be bothering you again," he said. He touched the woman lightly on the arm and walked around the house to his truck.

Tommy never played college football. In fact, it was a decade later before he earned a college degree from a little school in Oregon. He still returns to Alice for the Christmas holidays. He left his truck there, and his dad keeps it in good running condition.

Tommy's family doesn't see very much of him anymore, even during Christmas. All day long and well into the hours of the night he drives up and down those old dusty roads, out among the mesquite trees. He never married, and he says he never will, not till he finds his first true love. Her name was Julie.

Milk for Baby

Beeson's grocery was swarming with the usual Saturday morning crowd of town folks and farming families. When the front door opened and closed and no one appeared in the doorway, only Lawrence, the oldest son of William and Martha Beeson, seemed to notice. He peered over the counter and, seeing no one, shrugged his shoulders and returned to his task of sacking groceries for the steady flow of shoppers.

A moment later Lawrence spotted a young woman in a faded calico dress, weaving her way down the aisle. Her cheeks were gaunt, and her skin was pale as the white horse of death.

"I'm guessing she comes from a small truck farm,"

Lawrence thought to himself, noticing the tight hair bun that clung to her scalp.

When the woman reached the dairy cooler, she slid open the door and picked up a quart of milk. Carrying the milk bottle by the neck, she glided down the aisle. With each step the bottle bounced easily against her hip as she walked with her head down, never pausing.

All eyes turned to look at her when she stepped to the front counter. She looked so strange and out of place. The Beesons' oldest daughter, Alice, was the first to speak to her.

"Thirty cents, please," said Alice. The shoppers moved aside to allow her to pass. She nodded her head in gratitude and placed her milk bottle on the counter.

Her skin was the color of the milk, and when she lifted her pale face everyone gasped to see her eyes. They were blue as a cloudless sky, and pupil-less.

"Milk for baby, milk for baby, milk for baby mine," she said. Her voice was hoarse and whispery.

Alice knew she had no money, so she recorded the item on a slip of paper.

1 qt. of milk — 30 cents

"Please sign at the bottom," Alice said, turning the paper so the woman could read it and handing her a pencil.

Warily, the woman drew three circles and a line,

then turned and left the store.

Alice placed the paper under a drawer in the cash register. Though she had never seen the woman before, she knew she would see her again.

"She seemed so sweet and honest," Alice told her mother that night at the dinner table. "Somehow I knew she couldn't write."

"She was almost pretty," said Lawrence, "but her skin was so pale, and I've never seen eyes with no pupils."

The following Tuesday, Mrs. Beeson stood behind the counter when the woman appeared. She smiled and said, "Would you like to pay or sign for the milk?"

"Milk for baby, milk for baby, milk for baby mine," the woman said.

Mrs. Beeson wrote the item on a slip of paper.

1 qt. milk—30 cents

Sign here, please," she said.

The woman drew three circles and a line.

"There she is," the barber said, holding his clippers aloft and gazing across the street at Beeson's Grocery. He lifted the warm and steamy towel from Mr. Beeson's face and said, "See for yourself." From the barber's chair, Mr. Beeson watched the woman leave the store.

"She will be back," he said. He eased back into the chair and enjoyed the final moments of his weekly shave.

Wednesday came, and so did the young woman, leaving with another quart of milk beneath her arm. The next Saturday, with the bill now totaling more than a dollar, Mr. Beeson rose from the barber chair to follow her.

The barber handed him a towel and Beeson cleaned his face of shaving cream and exited the shop.

The woman turned a corner and climbed a small hill overlooking the growing city of Graham, Texas. She stepped from the sparsely traveled dirt road and slipped into the surrounding red oak woods. Mr. Beeson followed twenty yards behind, remaining unseen as she pushed open a heavy wrought-iron gate and entered a stagnant, moldy cemetery, with no apparent signs of any kind of life.

"Country people, those that were poor, were buried in this place," he thought.

The woman crossed the unkempt graveyard and knelt before a small, gray stone. Mr. Beeson kept a respectful distance and watched as the woman rolled over on her back and lay down on the grass above the grave.

Worried now that she was ill, he hurried to the grave. The woman seemed to be sinking into the ground. By the time Beeson reached the gravesite, she had disappeared, but he did see a small swatch of her calico dress as it slipped beneath the earth.

Beeson spotted the milk bottle and stooped to pick it up. Before his fingers reached the glass, the bottle sank into the ground. He drew in his breath and slowly stood to look about the cemetery, scanning the graves in a slow turn.

An hour later Beeson returned with the sheriff, a preacher, and two men from the barbershop. All but the preacher carried shovels.

"Are you absolutely certain of what you saw?" asked the preacher.

Beeson slowly nodded, and the men began to dig. When they reached the coffin, the sheriff lifted the pine lid.

The woman in the calico dress lay peacefully on her back. Her eyes were closed, and she was dead, but she was not alone. A baby curled up in her arms. The hem of the young woman's dress dipped into the mouth of the milk bottle.

The baby lifted her head and stared at the men. She

blinked her eyes and turned once more to suckle on the milk.

"I'll pay for the milk," said the preacher.

"No need for that," said Beeson. He lay on the ground and reached his hands into the grave. "My wife and I," he said, "would rather have the baby." They turned to go and did not see the smile on the woman's face.

Though the green of her calico dress
Would someday fade to gray
That smile on the dead woman's face
Would never go away.

Don't Fall in My Chili

Anybody who ever tried to stay in the old Jones place at night had troubles. They had troubles to begin with or they wouldn't be there in the first place. And the troubles only mounted once they got there. Before the sun came up, they'd be screaming and running for their lives. It always worked that way. Leastways it had till this story came to be.

The boy was poor, dirt poor. Anybody could see it by the hollow in his cheeks and the holes in his overalls. But he held himself with pride.

"Hmmm. He may be poor, but he's had good rearing," thought the grocer when the boy came into his store.

"What can I do for you, son?" the grocer said.

"I need a place to stay. My mule is tired," said the boy.

Looking over the boy's shoulder, the grocer thought, "More dead than tired." But he didn't say it, for he'd had good rearing, too. He knew the worst thing you could ever do was sass a person in need.

"There's only one place nearby," said the grocer. "It's good in some ways, bad in others."

"I like the good first," said the boy. "So give it to me good."

"The house is three miles to the west of town. The Jones place, if you're lost and have to ask. The Joneses all died long years ago. They died inside the house. It'll cost you not a penny. The water's good, as best I hear, and you can stay all night."

"So that's the good," the boy replied. "Now tell me 'bout the other."

"Hold on now, son," the grocer said. "There's more to the good. If you can stay the night, the place is yours. I've got the deed myself. Show up here tomorrow morning and the house, the farm, the barn, and the well, they'll all belong to you."

"Some things sound too good. They are balanced by the bad, I'll wager," said the boy.

His stock went up considerably with the grocer.

"I see you've learned some worldly ways. Now here's the bad. The house is haunted, son. It's best you know. You might consider moving down the road."

"Well, thank you for your warning, sir. I respect both the living and the dead. Each in his place, I've always said. Is there firewood at the old Jones place?"

"Oh, yes, well dried after all these years."

"Good," said the boy. "If I'm to stay the night, it passes best with chili. I'll need some fixins—meat, tomatoes, spices, and some onions."

"And beans for chili?" the grocer asked.

At this query, the boy looked the grocer in the eyes.

"I come from Texas, sir. I like the pinto bean as well as my neighbor, but never in my chili."

"Of course, just thought I'd ask," the grocer said.

His stock went up considerably with the grocer.

Just after sundown, the boy entered the Jones place. After starting a fire and browning the meat and onions, he settled back to watch his chili cook. Some hours later he filled his bowl. He was lifting the first spoonful to his mouth when he heard a terrible racket, something shaking in the chimney.

"I'm falling! I'm falling! Here I come."

The boy looked up the chimney and saw two skeleton legs dangling, legs without a body.

"It's all the same to me," said the boy. "Just don't fall in my chili."

Kerplunk! Two bony legs rolled out of the fireplace and scurried across the floor to the foot of the boy's chair. The boy went on eating his chili. But the racket came again, something shaking in the chimney.

"I'm falling! I'm falling! Here I come!" When he looked up the chimney, the boy saw two skeleton arms waving, arms without a body.

"Same as before," said the boy. "Just don't fall in my chili."

Kerplunk!

Two bony arms rolled out of the fireplace and skittered across the floor, laying themselves peacefully by the legs. The boy went back to eating his chili. But here it came again, like a hundred locomotives.

"I'm falling! I'm falling! Here I come!"

The boy looked up the chimney and saw a skeleton body. It was wiggling as best it could, without the use of arms and legs.

"Same as I told the rest of you," he said. "Just don't fall in my chili!"

Kerplunk!

With a grunt and a groan, the body landed on the floor. The boy watched it wiggle for a while. He saw it could go nowhere by itself. He put his bowl aside and carried the arms and legs to the skeleton body. If legs and arms could smile, these did. They also reattached.

The boy went back to eating his chili. But here it came again, shaking the rafters!

"I'm falling! I'm falling! Here I come!" When he looked up the chimney, the boy saw a skull, grinning somewhat stupidly.

"Just don't fall in my chili," said the boy.

Kerplunk!

The skull landed and rolled across the floor to join the rest of itself.

"Want some chili?" said the boy.

"I kinda lost my appetite," said the skeleton. "But mighty kind of you to ask. You seem a good-hearted fellow. How about I give you all my gold?"

"If that's your pleasure," said the boy.

"It's down in the cellar," said the skeleton.

When the boy opened the door to the cellar, it was dark and damp and smelled real funny, too.

"Don't think I want to go," he said.

"Let me guess," said the skeleton. "It's dark and damp and smells real funny, too. No problem." He broke a finger off and stuck it in the fire. The finger lit up like a candle, and he gave it to the boy.

Holding the finger before him, the boy walked down the stairs. There in the center of the cellar floor was a big bag of gold.

"Whoopee!" said the boy.

"Whoopee!" said the skeleton. "Now I can rest in peace. It's no fun haunting houses and guarding gold." And with that, he climbed back up the chimney and was gone.

The next morning, the boy walked in and told the grocer everything he'd seen.

"Sign here," said the grocer. "The house is yours."

The boy did, and as he turned to go, the grocer said, "Looks like we'll be neighbors, son. What might your name be?"

"Jack," said the boy.

His stock went up considerably with the grocer.

Knock! Knock!

Grandmother thought she heard knocking, but she couldn't be sure. All day the radio had warned of the hurricane coming. Howling winds and rain pounded against her house, and now this knocking sound.

When she opened the door, there in a puddle stood her grandson Phillipe, soaked to the skin.

"What are you doing here?" she asked. "Do your mother and father know where you are?"

"I walked here from school," said Phillipe. "I am running away from home."

"Well, you have come to a good place for running away. Come in and dry yourself off. What happened at school today?"

Phillipe took off his coat and shoes, but every layer of clothing was wetter than the layer before.

"The teacher gave me a note. She's mean to me."

"Let me see the note," Grandmother said. Phillipe handed her a crumpled sheet of pink school stationery. She read aloud, "Phillipe is stingy with the crayons and colored pencils. He is greedy. Please talk to him."

Grandmother looked at Phillipe with a scowl, though in her mind's eye she saw a sweet boy who needed a lesson.

"Hmmm, Phillipe. Let me make us some hot chocolate. And I will tell you what happens to greedy boys when they grow up."

Phillipe sat at the kitchen table while Grandmother spooned the chocolate in a pan of warm milk on the stove.

"It will only take a few minutes," she said. "Let me know when you see it boil." Then she turned to join him at the table.

"Where I come from, near New Orleans, there once lived a very mean and stingy old man. He had a daughter. She was young and beautiful, but he made her life miserable. There were only the two of them. Her mother had died.

"Every night the old man shut himself up in his room to count his money. If his daughter knocked on the door, like you knocked tonight, he wouldn't answer it. She would call, 'It is your daughter, Thérèse. Papa, it is Thérèse. Open the door.'

"He'd call to her, 'Go away! You are good for nothing. You only want to steal my money. Leave me alone.'

"Then he'd go back to counting his money, all those gold coins they say he had. She didn't care about his money. She was lonely. The old man wouldn't let her see anybody or have any friends at all.

"One night, on a night like tonight, she knocked at his door even louder than before. 'Papa,' she cried. 'It is your daughter, Thérèse. Help me, Papa. I am sick. Please, Papa, get a doctor for me.'

"He called to her, 'You are lazy. Don't bother me.'

"But Thérèse was very sick, and her fever grew as she stood outside his door. The old man fell asleep counting his money. The next morning he couldn't open the door. Something was blocking it. Do you know what it was?"

"Was it Thérèse?" Phillipe asked.

"Yes, it was Thérèse. But she was dead. It was her body."

"Grandmother, I think the milk is boiling." During the pause in the story, while Grandmother fixed the chocolate, the wind howled outside and thunder shook the house.

"Listen, Phillipe," Grandmother said. "It's fitting weather for a funeral."

"A funeral? Who has died?" Phillipe asked, his blue eyes round and full of fright.

"Thérèse has died, I told you. But her father was so

stingy with his money, he refused to buy her a vault to be buried in. No, he had them dig a hole for her and bury her in the soggy ground. But, Phillipe, you cannot do that in New Orleans. The ground is too low, below sea level in places. A coffin buried this way will float back to the surface. Do you like your chocolate? You are not drinking."

Phillipe nodded quickly and blew on his chocolate. The wind rattled the screen door as if someone were knocking.

"Do you hear it, Phillipe? The old man, Thérèse's father, he heard it too. On a night like tonight her coffin floated out of the ground. She lay cold on her back. Her skin was blue, but she floated in her coffin right to her father's door."

"Did she come out of the coffin?"

"Oh, no, Phillipe. Remember, she was dead. But the coffin knocked on the old man's door. The waves were washing it. Knock, knock, knock. Do it with me, Phillipe. Knock, knock, knock!"

"I don't want to," said Phillipe.

"It's only a story," said Grandmother. "A story about a stingy old man. Maybe he had been stingy as a boy, nobody knows. Anyway, he thought the knocking was the wind. Knock, knock. It was louder.

"He called to her, 'Go away, whoever you are.' But the knocking continued. Finally, the hurricane blew the coffin so hard, the old man heard a crash against his door. Splin-

ters flew, something was coming in! And, Phillipe, the wind sounded like a voice. The old man screamed. His eyes bulged out to see what he saw."

"What did he see?" asked Phillipe.

"Shhh! Sip your chocolate, and I will tell you." She took a sip herself and then continued.

"Three days later, when the hurricane had passed, the neighbors went to check on the old man. They found him dead. Thérèse's coffin had smashed through the door. Her body lay over the old man. Her skin was wet and soggy. And her fingers clutched his bag of money.

"They say there was enough money to buy a vault, a nice vault to bury the girl in. But the old man was buried in a wooden coffin, in a shallow grave. And on nights like tonight his coffin still floats. He comes knocking on the doors of stingy people."

"Grandmother."

"Yes, Phillipe."

"I won't be stingy anymore."

"I know, Phillipe. And neither will your children be. For now you know what happens."

Little Eight John

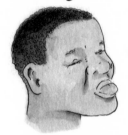

When Little Eight John's momma told him, "Don't," he did. When Little Eight John's momma told him, "Do," he didn't. He was as ornery a boy as ever tracked mud from the river bottom. Ain't nobody could ever figure him out.

"Little Eight John! Get yourself ready. We're going to church. It's about time to leave!" his momma called him in from playing. Here he come running.

"Wait for me, Momma. Oh, please don't go! You know how I love to go to church," Little Eight John said.

And the thing about it, he did love to go to church. He loved to catch the bugs and spiders and thousand-legged crawly things and mash 'em between the pages of the hymnbooks. He just loved doing stuff like that, sneaky stuff.

And on the way home his momma said, like she always did, "Little Eight John, you be careful and don't step on no toads or frogs or nothing like that. It'll bring bad luck on us all. You don't want that."

But Little Eight John did want that. It made him laugh and giggle just to see folks squirm in their misery.

"Yes, ma'am," Little Eight John would always say. "Can I go play by the bayou, if I don't get dirty, Momma?"

"If you don't get dirty," said his momma.

And off he'd go, looking for toads and frogs to stomp on. I know. That's bad. But that's Little Eight John. At least it used to be.

When his baby sister woke up with the whooping cough that very night, nobody knew what caused it. Nobody but Little Eight John, that is. He was laughing so hard he had to cover his head with a pillow to keep from being heard.

"And don't sit backwards in your chair, Little Eight John. Bad things gonna happen if you do."

"I won't sit backwards, Momma. I won't do that."

So, next day, with his momma cooking cornbread, Little Eight John turned around backwards in his chair. And even while she watched it, her cornbread burned to crispy black. Not even wild dogs ate it when she threw it over the fence.

And when his papa went to milk, the cow gave curdled milk.

And laugh, did Little Eight John laugh at that? You bet he did! All manner of warnings he ignored.

"Don't sleep with your head at the foot of the bed," his momma said one night. Better if she hadn't. "Make poor people of us all, that will."

Little Eight John couldn't wait to get to bed. Soon as the lights were out, he snuck around backwards and laughed himself to sleep.

Next morning all the hiding spots for money came up dry.

"Oh, Little Eight John, your family's poor. But at least nobody's dying. Best keep it that way. Little Eight John, don't go moaning and groaning on Sunday, whatever you do. That brings the Raw Head and Bloody Bones."

"Bloody Bones?" said Little Eight John.

"You heard me good, Raw Head and Bloody Bones. He'll eat you first and kill you later. He's nothing but bones, sloshing and dripping in blood, too mean for flesh to grow."

Little Eight John set to moaning that Saturday night, just to get a head start. For a month of Sundays, Mondays too, he groaned and moaned and carried on.

And then it happened. One night when he was home by

himself, Little Eight John heard a rustling in the trees out-side his window. He crawled out of bed just in time to see Old Raw Head and Bloody Bones slouching across the yard.

"Who you coming for?" said Little Eight John, but he knew.

Bloody Bones didn't say a word, just crept and crouched in from the woods, dripping blood all the way. Little Eight John crawled into bed and pulled his covers high and tight.

But that didn't do no good. Bloody Bones slipped up the side of the house and climbed through Little Eight John's window. He grabbed Little Eight John and shook him so hard he was nothing but a bloody spot. And on his way out the kitchen door, Bloody Bones wiped that spot on the wall.

The next morning, as she cleaned her kitchen, Little Eight John's momma saw that bloody spot. She wiped it with her cleaning rag, saying to herself, "I told that boy to wash his hands. Sometimes he just won't listen!"

And Little Eight John was no more.

He Came from the Grave

"My daddy says Mister Greech was the meanest man who ever lived," said Henry Sattler. Henry's head and arms poked out of the open end of his sleeping bag. His elbows propped up his chin as he spoke to his four best friends, Susan Tisdale, Jimmy Kramer, David Burton, and Merissa Sonfeld.

The five fifth graders lay with their sleeping bags facing a battery-operated lantern. Henry's father had placed the lantern in the darkest corner of the Sattler backyard. It was a chilly Friday in October, Halloween night. A backyard sleepover, with buckets of popcorn and a cooler of ice-cold root beer, had seemed like a good idea.

"My big sister says Mister Greech poured dirty dishwater on her and her friends one Halloween."

"What were they doing at his house anyway?" asked David.

"They didn't think he would be that mean," said Susan. "They rang his doorbell to Trick or Treat. He said, 'Wait a minute.' They thought he was bringing a kettle full of candy, but it was warm, dirty dishwater. He poured it all over them."

"Yuk!" said Jimmy.

"What did they do to trick him?" said David.

"Nothing," said Susan. "They were too scared. He had a dog he'd sic after kids."

"That dog was blind in one eye and limped along on three legs," Jimmy added. "But if he caught you, he would rip your clothes and chew your fingers off!"

"You're making that up!" said Merissa. Merissa was new to the neighborhood. Her father worked at the NASA Space Center. He had moved the Sonfeld family from Connecticut to Houston in June.

The four friends looked at each other and chimed in.

"We're not making anything up."

"Everybody knows about Old Man Greech."

"He was even mean to the mailman."

"And the trash pick-up man."

"And the meter reader."

"He was mean to everybody."

"Well," said Merissa, "if you're not making it up, you're exaggerating."

"Anyway," said Susan, "he can't hurt anyone now."

"Why not?" asked Merissa.

"He died last summer," said Henry. "He was watching television and just died."

"Probably watching some Freddy Krueger movie," said Jimmy.

"They found him the next day," Henry said. "Dead as a doorknob on his sofa. The television was still on."

"Guess we don't have to worry about Mister Greech anymore," David added.

"I wouldn't be too sure of that," said Jimmy.

"What do you mean by that?" the others said in unison.

"Well, my daddy says that if a ghost is ever coming back from the grave, it'll be on the first Halloween after he dies. He thinks Mister Greech might come back tonight. He'll be looking for anybody who ever made fun of him."

"I never made fun of him."

"Me neither."

"No way."

"I sure didn't. I was too scared to look at him."

"You are all being really immature," said Merissa. "Nobody is coming back from the grave."

"What makes you so sure?" said Jimmy.

"I'm just not afraid of ghosts."

"Okay," said Jimmy. "Mister Greech is buried in the cemetery over on Lexington Street, just four blocks from here. Why don't you go there and touch his gravestone if you're so brave?"

"I don't want to, that's why."

"Chick-chick-chick-chicken," said Jimmy.

The friends laughed and all reached for the popcorn bucket. As they were crunching and chewing the buttery kernels, Susan said, "It would be pretty cool to walk over to the graveyard tonight."

"Not me," said David. "I like it just fine in Henry's backyard." The others nodded their agreement.

"We shouldn't all have to go anyway," said Jimmy. "Merissa is the only one who's not afraid of Mister Greech. Maybe she can at least go touch his grave and come tell us about it."

"No!" said Susan. "She doesn't have to prove anything to us."

"Well, if you're not afraid, Merissa, what difference would it make?" said David.

"Yeah, and we could tell everybody at school about it Monday."

"I'll get in trouble if my parents find out anyone left the backyard," said Henry.

"So, we won't tell anybody," said Jimmy.

They all looked at Merissa. She spread her long, white

dress and said, "I would sure feel silly walking down the street in this." Thinking it was a costume party, Merissa had worn her Halloween outfit, a puffy floor-length Victorian-style dress.

"It's just a Halloween dress. Everybody will be dressed up tonight. You'll fit right in," said David.

"Merissa," said Susan. "Don't let them talk you into this."

"I think I want to do it," said Merissa. "They think I'm scared, but I'm not."

"That's good that you're not," said Jimmy, "because you can't just say you touched Mister Greech's grave. We need proof."

"What kind of proof?" said Merissa.

"You can get a knife and stab his grave. Then tomorrow morning we can get the knife."

"Where would I get a knife? I can't go home. They'd never let me back out."

"I can get one from the kitchen," said Henry. "But we have to return it first thing in the morning."

"Great," said Jimmy.

Henry climbed out of his sleeping bag and crossed the backyard. Soon he returned with a butcher knife. He held the blade high and made a few stabs in the air.

"Nice and sharp. Mister Greech is gonna love this in his chest."

"Don't say that!" said Susan.

"I don't mind," said Merissa. She took the knife and said, "How will I know where his grave is?"

"It's the only gravestone made of pink marble," said David.

"And it has an inscription about mourning. He mourned for his dog for the last years of his life."

"He mourns for that dog like a father for a child. That's what my mother used to say," said David.

"Okay," said Merissa. "I'll be back in half an hour. That is, unless Mister Greech grabs me and pulls me in."

"That's not funny," said Susan.

"Don't worry. I'll be back before you know it. Save me some popcorn." She crossed the yard, opened the gate, and disappeared from view.

"That was mean, Jimmy," said Susan.

"What?" said Jimmy. "She was the one bragging about not being afraid."

"She'll be fine," said Henry. "It's me I'm worried about." At that moment lightning flickered above them, quickly followed by a thunderous "Boom!" The four friends dived into their sleeping bags.

Merissa approached the cemetery with a slow and steady step. Though she tried not to make a sound, every footfall was punctuated with the crunching of dried leaves or the snapping of twigs. Billowy clouds floated quickly across

the sky, casting eerie shadows on the graveyard. Merissa paused at the heavy wrought-iron gate.

"Maybe I won't be able to open it," she thought. She lifted the latch and pushed with all of her strength, leaning her shoulder against the ironwork. The rusty hinges creaked in protest, then slowly gave way as the gate inched open.

The graveyard looked alive in the moonlight. A tall granite angel held her arm aloft. A young girl, carved in marble, stooped to pick a flower. Merissa took a deep breath and began walking with long, deliberate strides. She stepped from grave to grave, touching the tops of each tombstone as if to soothe the sleeping inhabitants.

"I will only be here for a few minutes. Then I'll leave you alone," she heard herself saying.

As if in reply, a clap of thunder shook the air. Merissa jumped and struck her knee against a marble slab. "Ohh!" she cried, then clamped her hand against her mouth. A gust of wind swept through the cemetery, twisting the trees into grotesque shapes.

Whoooosh! Wheeeee! went the wind, howling and moaning. Merissa imagined that people, dozens of dead people, were trapped in the trees. She shivered at the strangeness of the thought and wrapped her arms around herself.

"I can't do this," she called out. The wind replied with such fury she was flung to the ground. Merissa struggled to her feet. Her eyes stung with tears. Waving her arms in front of her, she began to run, blind to everything but the ground a few feet in front of her.

As suddenly as it began, the wind stopped.

Merissa rubbed her eyes. She turned in a slow circle, waiting for the next terror. Nothing happened. The cemetery lay in a dark and peaceful slumber. Merissa breathed easier. She cupped her hands around her eyes and squinted at the nearby graves.

In the shadow of a tall red oak twenty feet in front of her, she spotted a pink marble stone.

"Mister Greech," she said. "I think I have found you."

Merissa approached the stone and read the inscription.

Blessed Are They That Mourn
For They Shall Be Comforted
MERRIWEATHER GREECH
1907–1996

"He mourns for that dog like a father for a child," she said to herself. She knelt in front of the stone. Her right hand gripped the bone handle of Henry's knife. She lifted the blade from her sash and held it high over her head, clutching the knife handle with both hands.

"Uhhh," she whispered, shaking with fear. She closed her eyes and plunged the knife into the soft ground.

Mister Merriweather Greech lay silent in his grave, as

was expected. He was, after all, a dead man. Dead men do not cry out when their graves are stabbed, however rudely. Dead men do not thrust their arms through the ground and grab their tormentors. Dead men lie still as if nothing had happened.

For a brief moment, Merissa thought all was normal. She thought she would simply rise and join her friends. The wind was gaining strength once more. The tree limbs were waving. The air was howling, though softer than before.

The knife was already planted. Her deed was done. All she had to do was cross the graveyard, open the gate, and leave. She loosened her grip on the knife and stood, brushing her curls from her face.

"Well, that is done," she said. Only when she tried to take her first step did Merissa realize she might never leave the graveyard alive. She could not move.

"Ohhhh," she cried. "He has me! He has me! He is holding the hem of my dress!"

She fell to the ground in a sea of tears.

"Let me go. Please, please, LET ME GO!"

"She's been gone for over an hour," said Henry.

"Two hours and fifteen minutes, to be exact," said Susan.

"Should we go looking for her?" asked Jimmy.

"Huh? You go looking for her," said David. "I'm not going anywhere till morning."

No one spoke. Instead, Jimmy, Susan, David, and Henry ducked into the safety and warmth of their sleeping bags. Thankful that it was Merissa in the graveyard and not themselves, Merissa's friends drifted into innocent sleep. They awakened at 3:30 a.m. when the thunder roared and the pelting rain began.

"Is she here yet?" Jimmy whispered. When no one answered, he knew she had not returned.

"Maybe she went home," said David.

"I know I would," said Susan.

"I'm cold," said Henry.

"Me too."

"Same here."

"Yeah. She went home. Nobody would stay out in this weather."

The wind whirled and the lightning flashed and the four friends returned once again to their sleeping bags.

"Wow! That was some night," Henry said. The sun crept over the cold, wet yard. Car motors hummed to life. Newspapers thudded on doorsteps. Day was dawning on a sleepy Saturday. Merissa's four friends stuck their heads through the tent flap.

"Breakfast, anyone?" Henry's Mom called through the open kitchen window.

"Sounds like a winner," said David.

"Did you make your famous pancakes?" yelled Henry, proud that his mother made the best pancakes in the neighborhood.

"Strawberry pancakes okay with you?" she replied.

"Yeah!" came the cry of four hungry fifth-graders scrambling from their sleeping bags and splashing across the yard. Henry's mother opened the kitchen door.

"You kids look a sight," she laughed. "Where is Merissa?"

"She got scared and went home," said David. He looked to the floor and hoped his half-lie would be believed.

"That's funny," Henry's mother said. "Her mother called just twenty minutes ago wanting to be sure she was alright. I told her you were all still asleep. When did she leave for home?"

"She didn't exactly leave for home. Not from here anyway," said Susan.

"Henry?"

"Yes, Mother?"

"What is going on?" she asked. Henry looked at his friends for support. No one spoke.

"You children serve yourselves pancakes," Henry's

mother said. "Orange juice is in the refrigerator. Help yourselves. Henry, come with me. You have some explaining to do." She led him to the living room.

"Son, I don't want to embarrass you in front of your friends. You must tell me and tell me now. Where is Merissa?"

Henry swallowed before speaking. "She went to the graveyard last night," he said. "She never came back."

Ten parents arrived at the entrance to the Riverside graveyard in three vehicles. The gate was open. Merissa's mother screamed her daughter's name at the top of her lungs as she leapt from the car.

"Meri-ssssaaaaaa! Sweeeet baaaaby Meriiiiii-ssaaaa!" She sobbed and pulled at her hair with both hands.

They entered the gate and ran, as if on instinct, to the shadowy trees lining the graveyard. There, lying facedown at the base of a pink granite gravestone, was Merissa. She lifted her face to them.

"Don't come any closer," she said in a hoarse whisper. Her eyes loomed like deep, black holes on her pale skin. Thick globs of mud pasted her hair to her forehead. "Stay away. He will get you too." She pounded the grass with her fists.

"Merissa, what are you saying?" her father asked. "What do you think is happening?"

"He is dragging me into the ground, but you can still save yourselves. Leave me alone."

"Who?"

"Mister Greech. He has me. He will never let me go."

"Sweetheart, look behind you," her father said. "No one is holding you. Mister Greech is dead. When you plunged the knife into his grave, you stabbed the hem of your dress."

La Lechuza

In the south Texas town of Pleasanton, there stands a lone wooden bridge. Folks that live there call it, often in hushed tones, the Black Bridge. They tell their sons and daughters they should never wander outside at night near the Black Bridge. "If you do," the old ones say, "the *Lechuza* may come."

According to the stories, the *Lechuza* is an owl-like creature with the face of a shriveled old woman and the body of an enormous bird. She has wings where her arms should be and powerful claws on her feet, claws covered with crusted, dried blood!

There once was a young girl named Marcella who lived with her *abuela* in a tiny house on the far side of the Black

Bridge. They lived a simple life with no phone and no car, but the neighbors were kind and helped them when they needed it. They lived less than a hundred yards from the bridge and had to cross it to get to town.

As a child Marcella would play on the bridge, sometimes swinging on the rails, sometimes sitting and letting her legs dangle over the edge as she watched the dark and oily water far below. Sometimes she stayed too long.

"Marcella!" her grandmother would call. "It's getting dark. You hurry home!"

One Sunday Marcella's grandmother cooked her famous pork stew, and cousins and aunts and uncles by the dozens filled the backyard. As the evening settled, the children crowded into Marcella's room for short naps before the long walk home. They didn't sleep, of course, but listened to the stories through the open window.

"If you're foolish enough to be out at night on the Black Bridge, the *Lechuza* will soar over the tree tops and land behind you," said Tío Jorge.

"Then she'll laugh and curse. When you run, she'll chase you," said cousin Berto.

"She may get you with her claws!" laughed Jorge.

"*Siléncio!*" said Grandmother. "You know the children are awake and listening."

Though they laughed to think of scaring the children, there was no laughter later when they had to cross the Black Bridge. No one spoke as they hurried across the wooden planks. The adults walked near the edge to shield the children from falling, for the full moon looked alive on the oily water, shining and dancing, and the children loved to stare at it.

When everyone had gone, Grandmother came to Marcella's bedside.

"You were listening through the window, Marcella?"

"Yes. Was it true what they were saying about the Black Bridge, about the *Lechuza*?"

"Oh, *mi hija*. You must be careful of the Black Bridge. Never go there at night. People have seen the *Lechuza* there, sometimes in the early evening hours. She may look like she's just a big bird in the distance, instead of the wicked spirit she is."

"They say if you see her once, it could be accidental. Two times, it means bad luck. But if you see the *Lechuza* in the early evening hours three times, bad things can happen. Be very careful, *mi hija*. Your grandmother loves you."

"And I love you," Marcella said.

Marcella's *abuela* was in poor health, and one night she became very ill. Marcella grew afraid and decided to go to the neighbors for help. Her grandmother warned her not to go out in the dark.

"No, *mi hija*. Don't go out tonight. Remember the *Lechuza*!"

"Abuela, I'll be back soon," Marcella said. "I will only go to the neighbors for help. You need the doctor."

Marcella's grandmother pleaded with her, but she ran out the door and into the dark night. Soon she was at the nearest neighbor's house.

The lights were out, and no one answered when she pounded on the door. She ran to the next house, but again no one was home. Marcella walked to the center of the street. The neighborhood was dark and much too quiet.

Then she remembered about the wedding in San Antonio, some forty miles away. Everyone was gone to the wedding! They would not be back till the early morning hours. Marcella had to either return home without help or cross the Black Bridge and go into town.

It took her only a moment to decide. She would cross the Black Bridge carefully, then run to her cousin's house to call the doctor. It was a very still and ominous south Texas night. Marcella listened for the sound of wings in the air. Hearing nothing, she walked on.

With the bridge only a few feet in front of her, she heard a car. She saw headlights on the far side of the Black Bridge. Marcella's heart leapt, thinking it was one of her neighbors. When she heard the loud music on the car radio, she knew it wasn't a neighbor at all.

Marcella ran behind a tree and watched as the car stopped in the middle of the Black Bridge. Inside the car were two young men. She drew in her breath and hoped they hadn't seen her. The driver stepped out, waving his arms and shouting.

"Hey, Lechuza! Come get me! I'm not afraid of you! Hey, Birdwoman!"

He was taunting the *Lechuza*! The man on the passenger side tried to silence the driver, pulling at his sleeve to get him back in the car. The driver broke away and ran, still calling and waving his arms.

"Hey, Lechuza! You're not real! If you're real, come fight me!"

The man turned to his friend. "See? There is no birdwoman! It's only to scare the children."

The *whoosh* of enormous wings filled the air. Marcella looked up and saw a giant shadow fly over the car and land at the edge of the Black Bridge. In the headlights she could see the hideous face and shining yellow eyes of a snarling old woman. Her nose curved down like the beak of a hawk and large wings grew from her shoulders. Beneath the wings hung powerful claws, claws covered with crusted, dried blood!

The driver stood frozen for a second, then ran to his car. He yanked open the door, but the *Lechuza* was upon him before he could climb inside. His friend slammed the door and cowered in fear, while the *Lechuza* wrapped her claws around the driver's jacket.

As he scrambled to open the door, the *Lechuza* tore the jacket from him and soared high over the car, clutching the jacket in her claws. The driver leapt into the car and started the engine.

The night air burst with the screeching of tires and the smell of burning rubber as the car gained speed, but the *Lechuza* was not finished with the two men. From high overhead she dropped the jacket into the river and began a slow dive at the speeding car.

The *Lechuza* smashed into the windshield, shattering the glass and sending the car careening from one side of the bridge to the other. Marcella screamed, and the *Lechuza* turned her attention to the tree where Marcella lay crouched in fear. The car sped away, but the *Lechuza* did not follow.

For long minutes of silence Marcella hid in the shadows, listening to the *whoosh* of the *Lechuza*'s wings, close enough to rustle the leaves of the tree she hid behind. Terrified, Marcella stepped from her hiding place and ran in the direction of her house, fearing that at any moment she might feel the bite of the birdwoman's claws.

In her mad dash to safety, she could not distinguish the wind of her running from that of the *Lechuza*'s wings. Cutting through the backyard of a neighbor, she stumbled over a pile of firewood, and as she scrambled to her feet she heard the screech of the *Lechuza*.

"*Qué milagro!*" Marcella shouted, entering the safety of her home. She locked the front door and pulled a dresser in front of it. Then she went to her grandmother's bedside and told her everything.

As she finished her story, Marcella became aware of a faint scratching sound on the roof of the house.

"Grandmother! It has found me!"

The scratching became louder. The *Lechuza* was on the roof of the house trying to get in! Marcella helped her grandmother roll off the bed. Together they hid in the closet, closing the door behind them and piling blankets on top of themselves.

As the scratching grew louder and more frantic, Marcella's grandmother prayed for protection. Over and over Marcella saw the image of the *Lechuza* in her mind.

When the scratching sound reached its most deafening level, it suddenly stopped. Marcella and her grandmother waited and listened.

Finally, Marcella opened the door of the closet. She saw a pale ray of sunlight coming through a window. The *Lechuza*, a creature of darkness, had disappeared with the sunrise.

The very next Sunday Marcella's grandmother cooked her famous stew again. The chunks of pork were smothered in thick, brown gravy, as always. Family was gathered, as always, but something was different this time. Grandmother instructed the cousins to drag a ladder to the house and lean it against the roof. Then, one by one, she made the teasing, taunting men climb the roof to see the deep scars cut in the shingles.

"These cuts were made by the claws of the *Lechuza* as it

tried to enter my house and get Marcella and myself. You must never again doubt that the *Lechuza* is real. You must never taunt her. You must never go near the Black Bridge after dark!"

Now, if you go down to that old house near the Black Bridge and climb to the roof, you'll see those long, deep scratches. You might think it curious that there would be scratches where there are no trees close enough to touch the roof with their branches.

If you do travel south of Pleasanton, and if you decide to cross the Black Bridge, don't go at night. You may meet the *Lechuza*!